主題樂園
幻想工程挑戰賽
MAKING WORLDS:
AN IMAGINEERING
PROJECT

圖錄
Plates

相信青年的無限可能
朝由共識形成的主題樂園邁進
台北當代藝術館館長／駱麗真

本館從 2021 年起推出的「青年策展人計畫」，鼓勵支持年輕策展工作者，以及剛踏入策展領域的策展人，能夠於專業正式的展覽平台，發表分享個人獨到的見解與專業。首屆「青年策展人計畫」邀請黃又文、馮馨與彼勇・依斯瑪哈單等三位策展人，從現實社會、科技視角及原民力量討論出發，舉辦展覽「為了明天的進行式」，充滿創意及新世代的觀察，後續為展覽帶出多重極具意義的討論。今年，「青年策展人計畫」由策展人孫以臻的「共識覺」與王韓芳「主題樂園幻想工程挑戰賽」分別於館內一、二樓舉行。

孫以臻、王韓芳兩位策展人都具有科學學習的背景，孫以臻大學主修生物科學，後續轉往藝術策展領域，從她過往策劃的展覽可以看到許多跨領域結合科學思維與藝術表現的內容。本檔「共識覺」當中，策展人邀請六位／組國內外藝術創作者，從「人類的共識如何達成？」這個富含直覺的提問出發，拉出人類與非人類、人類與異世界當中，關於社會政治與科技發展等相互映照的關係。策展人王韓芳則從社會樂園化的面向切入，在「主題樂園幻想工程挑戰賽」將六位不同國家的藝術家比擬為迪士尼樂園當中的幻想工程師，在策展人所建構起的環境內，觀眾帶著既像勞動者又似表演者的多元身分，隨著動線穿梭在每件藝術作品及空間元素當中，逐步揭露這座去脈絡化的主題樂園所展現及形構的社會運行機制和方法，映照出一片有別日常的平行宇宙。

本檔展覽感謝許多贊助單位的共同支持：THERMOS 膳魔師、當代藝術基金會、財團法人紀慧能藝術文化基金會、老爺會館、台灣愛普生科技股份有限公司、台灣索尼股份有限公司、中央廣播電台、國立臺北藝術大學關渡美術館、臺北市立建成國中、台北電影節、Yogibo、奧地利聯邦總理府藝術文化、公共服務暨運動部（Federal Ministry for Arts, Culture, Civil Service and Sport, Republic of Austria）等單位，在諸方共識相互凝聚下，於本館順利創造出一座現實與虛構並存的主題樂園。

Believe in the Infinite Possibilities of Young Talents — Towards the Theme Park Formed by Co-consciousness

Director of MoCA TAIPEI / Li-Chen Loh

Since 2021, MoCA TAIPEI initiated the Emerging Curator Program to encourage emerging curators to present their insights and profession through a professional exhibition platform. In the first year of the Emerging Curator Program, MoCA TAIPEI invited three curators—Erica Yu-Wen Huang, Feng Hsin and Biung Ismahasan to present the exhibition *Tomorrow, Towarding*, tackling issues from different angles, ranging from realistic society and technology to indigenous power. With innovative and new generation perspectives, the exhibition generates meaningful and multifaceted discussions. For this year, the curators of MoCA's 2022 Emerging Curator Program—Yi-Cheng Sun and Wang Han-Fang, bring us the exhibitions *The Proto-ocean for Co-consciousness* and *Making Worlds: An Imagineering Project*, which were held at MoCA's exhibition galleries respectively at first floor and second floor.

Yi-Cheng Sun and Wang Han-Fang are both with background of learning science. Yi-Cheng Sun majored in Life Science and later turned to curating. From past exhibitions she has curated, we could see many works with cross-disciplinary content combining science and art. In the exhibition *The Proto-ocean for Co-consciousness*, the curator invites 6 artists/ artist collectives and begins with the instinctive question— "How do we bring about the co-consciousness?" underlining the relationships between the social political and scientific development in the human/ nonhuman, human/heterogeneous world. The curator Wang Han-Fang explores the Disneyfication of the society and pictures 6 participating artists as imagineers of the theme park. In the environment built by the curator, members of the audience are like laborers and performers; they follow the designated traffic flow and pass through each artwork and spacial element, and gradually disclose the mechanisms and methods that the decontextualized theme park has presented and formed.

The exhibitions are made possible thanks to our sponsors: THERMOS; Contemporary Art Foundation; Ji Huei-Neng Art and Culture Foundation; Royal Inn, Epson Taiwan; SONY; Radio Taiwan International; Kuandu Museum of Fine Arts, Taipei National University of the Arts; Jian Cheng Junior High School; Taipei Film Festival; Yogibo; Federal Ministry for Arts, Culture, Civil Service and Sport, Republic of Austria, and more. By forming co-consciousness with multiple people involved, MoCA TAIPEI has successfully created a "theme park" in which reality and imagination coexist.

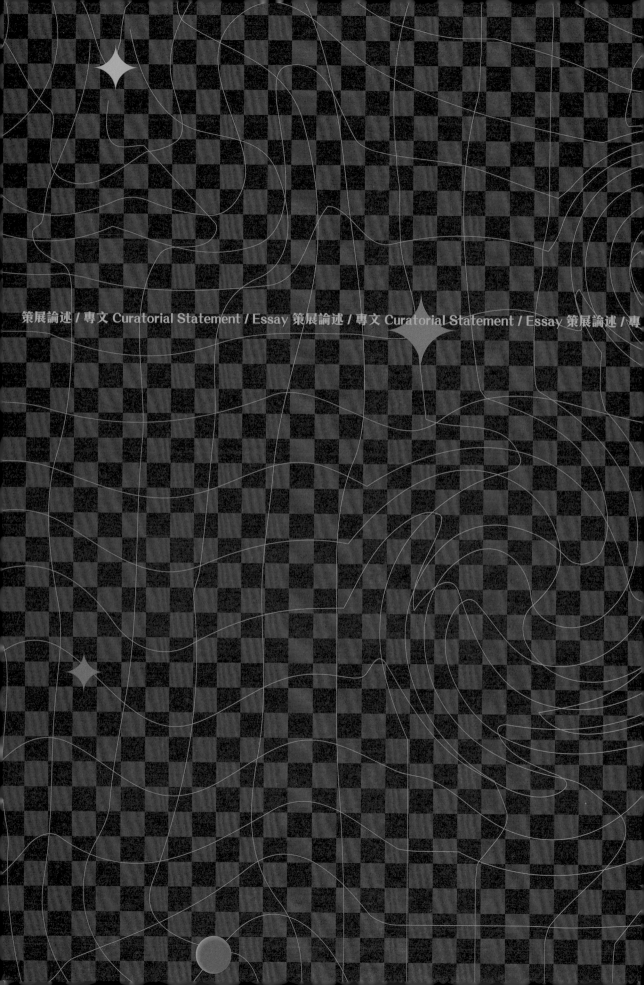

策展論述 / 專文 Curatorial Statement / Essay 策展論述 / 專文 Curatorial Statement / Essay 策展論述 / 專

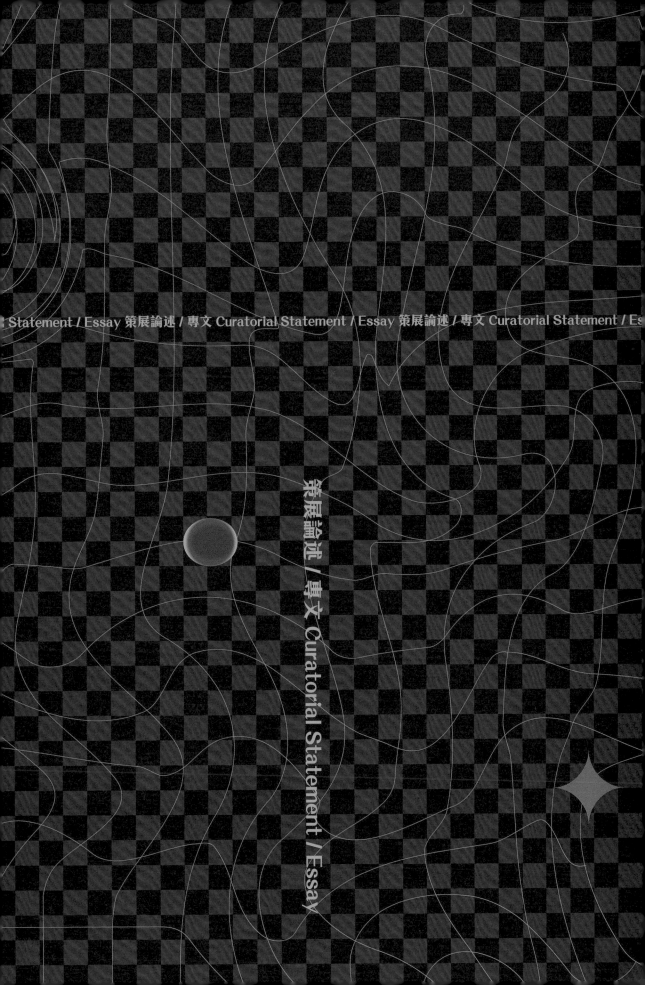

策展論述 / 專文 Curatorial Statement / Essay

每個目的地都是每個地方，而每個地方也成為了每個目的地
一元的消費者
慶祝製造變成了製造慶祝
製作人成為消費者
循環的面向學

迪士尼主題樂園的歷史背景

1955 年，華特・迪士尼（Walt Disney）在加州創建了第一座現代化主題樂園—迪士尼樂園。所謂主題樂園，就是園中從空間安排、場景轉換、動線規劃、視聽影音至角色活動都集中表現一個或幾個特定的主題故事，以再現某些現實無法抵達的場景，滿足遊客脫離當下並進入幻想世界遊樂的渴望。

1964 年發生於紐約世界博覽會，是迪士尼樂園再進一步的重要事件。當時華特・迪士尼受邀為奇異公司、百事可樂及福特汽車發展裝置，在當屆世博描繪科技進展與人類文明高度相關的期待之下，產生了「進步的旋轉木馬」（Carousel of Progress）、「這是一個小小世界」（It's a Small World）及「魔法飛車」（Magic Skyway）等設施，爾後部分的設施也遷移至園區內常駐。後續 80 年代更發展出在概念上相關聯的 EPCOT 主題園區（Experimental Prototype Community of Tomorrow），[1] 融和人類科技成就及 11 個國家的景觀與文化元素，以「未來生活」與「世界之窗」創造許多體驗式的場景，號稱為永遠的世界博覽會。

上述這些來自電影場景、歷史街道，又或是各國文化景觀的陳列，在風格化的主題樂園情境塑造中，似乎就像一層平行的膜覆蓋於真實空間之上。它們透過有功能性的跨媒介空間敘事，統合地提供一個沉浸式的幻境給每位來訪的遊園客，並巧妙地改造了幻境與真實空間之間的關係連結與意義指涉。本展則是希望藉由思考主題樂園的系統模式，探尋當主題樂園離開了園區而進入社會情境之中，它的生產技術及與社會之間的關係為何？進而思索作為一般遊園客的個人，又該以什麼角色或身份，去玩這場日常遊戲。

社會的迪士尼化：何處不是主題樂園？

借用美國社會學學者 Alan Bryman 曾在其著作《社會迪士尼化》（The Disneyization of Society）提出的論點，「社會的迪士尼化」意指主題樂園的運行模式於各領域滲透且日益增長擴大的現象。無論是餐廳、飯店、購物中心，又或是歷史遺跡保存、美術館及博物館，都可見其蹤跡。它常是一個高度商業化且具高度控制性的空間，也同時是一個全心全意取悅消費者的空間，能不斷地自我繁殖且廣受市民喜愛。而迪士尼化的重要要素包含：主題化（theming）、混種消費（hybrid consumption）、授權商品化（merchandising）及勞動力表演化（performative labour）。「主題化」指的是以故事去統轄空間，故事成為空間的一種敷面及材料；而「混種消費」我認為則是對於「商品」的重新定義，「商品」不再等同於「產品」，買賣將離開產品製造，而進入消費者的體驗塑造；至於「授權商品化」暗示的是，傳統自然資源的典範轉移，新

興市場在於「人類」自身的個資、著作財產及新型態的勞動力。這也導致勞動力表演化的討論，意即，面對消費者的服務工業將被視為是一種表演工作，以劇場的方式提供服務以成立一個與眾不同的消費體驗。

所以，社會的迪士尼化會帶來什麼情境？我認為它會帶來如萬花筒一般的具現化分眾世界。同一文本會依據不同目標與需求分化為不同的劇本，自主題概念進到實際空間中，從入口坡道的角度、門口懸吊的招牌警語至每個服務人員的動作表情，將成為一部完整劇本的各個環節，妥善思考著遊園客被預期的遊歷經驗及各種預設動作。而也正因同一文本會依據不同目標與需求進行分化，為了能有足夠的適應彈性及滿足大量開採的需求，容易導致故事版本被簡化、片面化及公式化，成為一種重覆的無限循環，最後只剩下感官刺激與娛樂消費，而喪失了意義生產。這些被具象化、物質化的主題概念，夾帶著轉換為五感經驗的宣傳思維，自意識型態變身為真實空間形式的世界，將更為挑戰在沉浸空間中個人的自主判斷，及對於事實／現實的多重理解，就像是創造了多個微型人造新世界，不斷地引誘著我們。

敘事空間與技術

此展中，除了有關社會迪士尼化中對於主題化背後意識型態的思考與討論，也同時有一條交錯的伏線在嘗試理解 20 世紀後敘事的空間轉向，及上述各種敘事空間中的敘事方法、技術及政治。一種帶著特定意圖、商品化、遊戲化的空間，通過敘事的手法來編排場景序列，以期展開一個富有感染力的場所，同時也成為一種敘事語言，一個日常表演的舞台。

在這些場景搭建的過程中，以幻想工程為例，皆可看見因應主題性「去脈絡」及「再脈絡」的狀態，而在幻想工程師的說法中則可視為「改編」（reprogramming）。若我們以迪士尼樂園中的設施「陰陽魔界：驚魂古塔」（The Twilight Zone: Tower of Terror）為例，[2] 1980 年代原取材自經典電視劇《陰陽魔界》的故事背景，場景設定於 30 年代好萊塢華麗風格式的飯店，借用《陰陽魔界》中墜入第五維度的概念，描述一個雷電交加的夜晚，被劈中的建築物將部分消失的驚悚故事。也因此，遊樂設施以飯店中的電梯為主體，載著遊園客失重式下墜作為運動方式，以達成遊園客「驚聲尖叫」的行為目標。搭建像這樣的敘事空間，敘事材料含括不同時間向度、地理位置及各式媒介等材料拼貼，有 30 年代好萊塢飯店奢華的 Art Deco 建築樣式、螢幕畫面中以數位技術及配音死而復生的主持人羅德·塞林（Rod Serling）、現場扮演飯店接待員的迪士尼工作人員及各式各樣能夠影響事件走向的物件，形成各個場景貫串於這個垂直下墜的運動過程之間，以期完整化遊客「驚恐尖叫」的娛樂目標。

爾後，在 2022 年陣亡將士紀念日之際，因應新設施開幕的需求，同時也借勢宣傳新上映的電影《星際異攻隊 #2》，這個敘事空間被改編（reprogram and reskin）為《星際異攻隊》中收藏家（the Collector）的堡壘（因該設施外牆裝飾物下的建築結構近似軍事堡壘），重生為另一個以「歡樂式的尖叫」為主軸的敘事空間。另在海的他端的東京迪士尼樂園，因亞洲市場並不熟悉《陰陽魔界》的故事文本，而轉用海洋探險主題及受詛咒的雕像進行重編。同樣的案例也發生於另一個經典設施「飛濺山」（Splash Mountain），因應全球反種

族歧視運動，由《南方之歌》的故事背景改編至第一個由黑人女性為主角的動畫《公主與青蛙》。這些由幻想工程所搭造的敘事空間中，可見過往城市、歷史、文化、文本等敘事素材，藉由著跳躍、錯位、拼貼、重組等編輯工程在不同內容或物質媒介上混和搭建場景，加上娛樂及表演化的勞動形式，依循著不同目的：懷舊、娛樂、清洗、消費、政治等，精準設定路徑、經驗及預期效果，再授權並複製、微調及黏貼於其他情境。整個世界就像是一幅全球拼貼畫，由脫離語境的各種碎片組成，且不斷地運動著。

有意思的地方在於，這樣編排的方式一方面稀釋了敘事空間的線性（時間性），而以某種近似「主題大街」的櫥窗式空間串聯場景，又或是以一個遊戲或娛樂策略式的目標進行場景連結。似乎，在這樣的敘事空間中，與因果邏輯高度關聯的時間性敘事在整體中將被局部化，而與場景調度相關連的空間性敘事將成為整體的基礎結構，同時開放性地邀請促發事件的參與者共同參與、製作及消費。這樣的時間和空間敘事的結合（space-time coordinates），在敘事空間的場景搭建過程中，因應遊園客身體及主觀視角的加入，現場性的各種敘事技術及物件將擔負更重要的角色，如：聲音表情、肢體語言、攝影、動態影像等具有現場性的手勢，企求由遊歷經驗對敘事所生產的認知、解釋及意義能順理成章地發生，進一步促使觀眾產生被預期的行為。至於敘事意義的產生，也變得更為流動，因應著各個拼貼的碎片在敘事空間各個不同時空的連接與分離，在主觀的視角下階段性地產生，爾後又消失再進到下一個時空狀態。

轉換位置：將來玩家的角色

也因此，也許我們可以說，主題環境給予遊園客們一個機會集體性地也身體性地進入他者的思想領域—世界。相比於基礎建設，它可能更像是一種意識形態的建設，藉由主題故事化作物質性的敘事空間，以傳達意欲傳播的意念或行為。那麼遊園客在其中將成為什麼樣的角色？按照劇本玩遊戲的玩家？又或是企圖尋找出錯點的玩家？當這樣的主題環境自遊樂園區擴延至社會，並成為一個自給自足的世界時，是否娛樂與遊戲將成為新的日常，遊戲規則成為新的日常律法？這次的展覽，以一個「幻想工程」挑戰的意念，邀請藝術家們玩轉「工程」的系統與機制，但企求轉向「幻想」的目的，並期待觀眾在過程中挑戰「玩家」的位置。

當敘事已成為可供玩樂的形式，各種個體／群體敘事、新聞傳播、文化文本又或是政治宣傳都可以短影像、電影，更甚是一個主題式的樂園空間來進行更有力的表述。敘事也因此成為一種行為及遊戲，被放入了玩（娛樂式的體驗）之中，而它也終將系統化、模組化，成為一個可以被複製的規則，就如同迪士尼樂園的設計一般。飽含遊樂性的敘事空間提供一個更加動態的系統，人們將在娛樂經驗中工作、交流、消費、娛樂、學習、抗爭，更甚是戀愛。所以作為玩家，除了照著劇本運動、探索、操縱與被操縱，因其具備的互動、開放與流動的特質，若我們如幻想工程師一般思考，成為系統的共同設計者，將使玩家自被動改為主動的角色，便有機會培養我們如同理解文學劇作、當代藝術又或是電影一般，成為主題樂園系統中能夠辨識深意並創造意義的遊園客。

在這裡你將會離開現實的今日，
而進入一個昨日、明日與夢想的世界 [3]

---

[1] EPCOT 的名字來自華特・迪士尼一個早年沒有成真的構想。EPCOT 計畫原計將迪士尼樂園發展至都市規劃的規模，藉由建立一座擁有頂尖先進科技的小型城市，人們可以在裡面生活、工作、和創造，成為引領世界的實驗原型城市。

[2] 《陰陽魔界》改編的資料參考自迪士尼出版的紀錄片《Behind the Attraction》第一季第 4 集。

[3] 此句話來自華特・迪士尼，常被設置於迪士尼園區的入口處。

Making Worlds: An Imagineering Project

Every destination becomes every place,
and every place becomes every destination
monadic consumer
celebration of the production turned into production of the celebration
producer-turned-consumer
facets of circulation

The History of Disneyland

In 1955, Walt Disney founded Disneyland, the world's very first modern theme park. A theme park, by definition, is an amusement park where space design, foot traffic flow, mise-en-scènes, audiovisual experiences, characters, and activities all revolve around one or several themed stories, transporting the visitor to a world of fantasy through fanciful settings.

The 1964 New York World's Fair saw Disney take an ambitious step further. He had been invited to create installations for General Electric Company, Pepsi-Cola, and Ford Motor Company. With the fair's mission in mind to present technological progress that would transform the face of human civilization, Disney's WED Enterprises designed and created Carousel of Progress, It's a Small World, and Magic Skyway. Some of the installations were later moved to other Disney theme parks as permanent exhibits. Conceived later in the 1980s, EPCOT, or Experimental Prototype Community of Tomorrow[1] celebrates humanity's technological innovation, and encompasses the landscapes and cultures of 11 countries. Featuring pavilions that provide immersive and interactive experiences exploring life in the future and in other parts of the world, EPCOT is dubbed the "permanent world's fair."

These stylized displays of film settings, historic street scenes, or cultural landscapes of different countries are the result of a transdisciplinary spatial narrative that serves a particular purpose: conjuring an immersive fantastic environment for each visitor, where, much like a parallel universe, all connections between this land of fantasy and the real world dissolve, relationships reconfigured. Examining the mechanism of a theme park, *Making Worlds: An Imagineering Project* investigates the relationship between society and the production technology of a theme park in a social context, as well as the role of the individual as a visitor and player.

The Disneyization of Society: Theme Parks Everywhere

The construct of Disneyization was proposed by American social research scholar Alan Bryman in his book *The Disneyization of Society* (2004), where he described it as "the process by which the principles of the Disney theme parks are coming to dominate more and more sectors of American society as well as the rest of the world." Whether in restaurants, hotels, shopping malls, historic sites, or museums, Disneyization is everywhere. Often a highly commercialized, controlled space dedicated to pleasing consumers, a theme park tends to self-replicate, and enjoys universal popularity. The four dimensions of Disneyization include: theming, hybrid consumption, merchandising, and performative labor. Theming is where a space is dominated by a narrative that serves as a material mostly unrelated to the space to which it has been applied. Hybrid consumption, in my opinion, refers to the redefining of merchandise, where merchandise no longer equals product; transaction no longer involves manufacturing of goods, but of consumer experiences. As for merchandising, it suggests a paradigm shift in traditional natural resources: the emerging market lies in people's personal information, intellectual property, and new forms of labor. This leads to the idea of performative labor, where frontline service work is seen as a labor of performance, which renders service in a theatrical manner to create a unique consumer experience.

What does the Disneyization of society bring? I think it brings a kaleidoscopic world manifested in niche markets. The same narrative is differentiated into different scripts according to objectives and needs: from the theme to the physical space, from the slope of the entrance ramp, the warning sign hanging at the door, to the movements and facial expressions of each staff member. These elements coalesce into one comprehensive script where visitor experience and behavior analysis are carefully considered. Because the same narrative is differentiated, to achieve maximum adaptability and satisfy the goal of reconceptualization, mass replication, and mass dissemination, versions of the story become simplified, one-sided, and formulaic, repeating in an endless loop where nothing is left but sensory stimuli, entertainment, and consumption, lacking ultimately in significance. These visualized and materialized theme concepts, conceived with propaganda in mind to create sensory experience, translate from ideology to physical form. Such immersive worlds of fantasy challenge the visitor's sense of judgment and their multiple understandings of fact/reality, beguiling them into these shiny, human-made microcosms.

Narrative Space and Technology

This exhibition not only investigates the ideology behind theming in the Disneyization of society, but attempts to unravel the post–20th-century narrative, where the focus shifts from temporality to spatiality, as well as the above-mentioned methodology, technology, and politics in various narrative spaces. Such a narrative space—constructed with a specific intent, commodified, gamified, enlivened by meticulously orchestrated settings — aims to create an immersive experience while becoming itself a form of narrative language, a stage for everyday performance.

In the process of building these scenes, take Imagineering for example. Decontextualization and re-contextualization as a response to a particular theme is a classic approach, or "reprogramming," to borrow from Imagineering lingo. If we look at the Twilight Zone: Tower of Terror,[2] a facility in Disneyland, which was adapted from a 1980s television series of the same name, the horror story takes place at a 1930s glam-style hotel where part of the building hit by lightning on a stormy night vanishes into thin air, and people in the hotel fall into the fifth dimension, an idea borrowed from the original series. The highlight of the amusement facility is the elevator in the hotel, which carries passengers up high and drops them in a free fall, allowing them to scream their lungs out, achieving the objective of the ride. To create a space such as this requires varying narrative elements: time dimensionality, geographic location, and different mediums, including Art Deco architecture reminiscent of the 1930s glamour, a Rod Serling resurrected with digital technology and voice-over on the screen, Disney staff members who play the hotel receptionists, as well as countless objects which change the direction of events. The diligently choreographed scenes culminate with a final free fall that both terrifies and entertains visitors in fright and delight.

For Memorial Day Weekend in 2022, this space—reprogrammed and reskinned into The Collector's Fortress as part of the promotional campaign for the movie *Guardians of the Galaxy Vol. 2*, because the lower part of the building façade resembled a military fortress— had transformed into another narrative space with the same mission: to excite shrieks of glee. Across the ocean, Tokyo Disneyland reprogrammed the Twilight Zone into a sailing adventure with a cursed statue due to the Asian market's unfamiliarity with the story. A parallel example can be found in another classic facility Splash Mountain, where in response to the global anti-racism movement, the background had been changed from *Song of the South* (1946) to *The Princess and the Frog* (2009), the first animation film that features a Black female protagonist. In these Imagineered spaces, one thing is clear: narratives of different cities, histories, and cultures are reconfigured through spontaneous arrangement, dislocation, mélange, and reorganization of scenes, ultimately enacted with labor in the form of entertainment and performance. These said narratives serve the purpose of nostalgia, recreation, ideological campaign, consumerism, and politics, laboriously calibrated to designate foot traffic flow, tailor visitor experience, and create anticipated effects, followed by international franchise deals. A global mosaic of fragments out of context, forever in tectonic shifts.

Fascinatingly, this arrangement disrupts the temporality of the narrative space, where a Main Street (like in Disneyland) serves as the central passageway that leads to different scenes (such as Adventureland, Tomorrowland, or Frontierland), each designed with a game/entertainment-oriented strategy. In such a space, it appears, the highly causal temporal narrative is marginalized, while the spatial narrative, the product of a carefully crafted mise-en-scène, underlies the entire story, where participants who trigger the events are invited to engage, produce, and consume. In the construction of a narrative space following such space-time coordinates, the physical perception and vantage point of the visitor come into play. Different on-site narrative tactics and objects become crucial. Tangible techniques, from facial expression, body language, photography, to videography, are applied to elicit a predictable reaction to the narrative from the visitor, including their understanding and interpretation of the events, as well as their acknowledgement of the events' significance. Eventually becoming fluid, the meaning of the narrative sees itself in fragments, scattered and reassembled in different contexts and cast in subjective perspective, dissipating before emerging in another space-time dimension.

Switching Positions: The Future Role of the Player

Perhaps we could say, a themed environment allows visitors to collectively and physically enter the thought domain—the world— of another. Compared with infrastructure, a themed environment is more akin to a constructed ideology, where a theme, adapted from a story, materializes into a narrative space in an attempt to convey an intended idea or encourage a certain behavior. What, then, is the role of the visitor? A player who sticks to the script of the game? Or a player who seeks to locate a bug? When a themed environment such as this expands beyond an amusement park and spreads its tentacles across society, becoming a world unto itself, will games and entertainment be the new everyday, and the rules of the game, society's new regulations? *Making Worlds: An Imagineering Project* invites the artists to challenge the engineering mechanism with the purpose of imagination, while engaging the viewer as a player.

When narrative has become a form of entertainment, everything from individual/collective narrative, news broadcast, cultural narrative, to political propaganda can transform into a compelling statement through video clips, movies, even theme parks. Narrative, in a sense, is reinvented into a type of behavior and game, configured into the entertainment experience of play, where it will inevitably be systematized and modularized into a rule that can be replicated, just like the design of Disneyland. An entertainment-oriented narrative space provides a more dynamic system. It is a place where people work, socialize, consume, play, learn, protest, even fall in love in their experience of entertainment. As players, apart from moving, exploring, maneuvering, and being maneuvered according to the script, we could actually take advantage of the interactive, open, and fluid nature of the game, where we are free to co-design the system like Imagineers, going into active rather than passive mode. There is a chance, in the similar way we approach literature, theater, contemporary art, or cinema, we could reimagine ourselves with a discerning eye, who with a wave of their hand conjures meaning from the depths of the theme park system.

Here you leave today
and enter the world
of yesterday, tomorrow
and fantasy[3]

¹ EPCOT is inspired by an unrealized concept of the same name developed by Walt Disney. The idea was to develop a planned community, much like a small city with cutting-edge technology where people could live, work, and create. EPCOT was originally intended to be an experimental prototype city ahead of its time.

² *The Twilight Zone* adaptation references episode 4, season 1 of Behind the *Attraction*, a Disney+ documentary TV series (2021).

³ A quote from Walt Disney, it is often inscribed on a plaque hung above the entrance of Disneyland.

進入故事，成為其他：
「主題樂園幻想工程挑戰賽」
裡的動態影像裝置與新敘事主義實踐

若要將「旅途」的感官經驗確實傳遞給觀者，就不能將故事說得太完整、太絕對，絕對到讓觀者只能當個單純的窺視者。旅途必須由觀者來完成、來體驗，觸感空間若無肉身作為媒介，也就不再有深化、延展的可能。
——江凌青，〈當代影像的命運：從琳賽·席爾的創作觀察當代錄像裝置對電影美學的擴延與回返〉，2011。

● 成為其他

身為九〇年代出生的人，在義務教育的歲月裡，套裝式的畢業旅行絕對少不了本地主題樂園的「山六九」[1] 行程。因為主題樂園需要購買大量的土地，它們往往坐落在遠離城市的郊區戶外，是使人前往另一現實的娛樂城堡，以複雜的硬體結構製造的遊樂設施，創造各種刺激的身體感，吸引遊客與親友一起體驗。但這一切，都比不上迪士尼樂園或環球影城的魅力。它們更是以多種方法體驗多種敘事的載體，故事讓人著迷其中。

由安東尼・霍普金斯在《西方極樂園》中飾演的福特博士，給了我們一個關於主題樂園作為擬像為何充滿魅力的解釋：

「他們（消費者）回來是因為微妙之處、細節。他們回來，是因為他們發現了一些他們認為以前沒有人注意到的東西⋯⋯一些他們已經愛上的東西。
他們不是在尋找一個告訴他們自己是誰的故事，他們已經知道自己是誰了。
他們來這裡，是因為他們想一睹自己成為其他人的潛力。」

這番話道出了布希亞談論擬像與消費時的思考：在《物體系》的視角中，消費並不是一種物質的實踐，也不是「豐產」的現象學。消費與購買、擁有、花費與享受不同，不在於我們買的衣服、食物、汽車，而是在於把所有上述的元素組織為表達意義功能的實質。消費是一個虛擬的全體，一種記號的系統化操控活動，物則意味著使消費者個性化、或說產生差異性的記號。布希亞將消費理解為永不滿足的欠缺、完全唯心的作為，克制或規範它則是一種天真或荒謬的道德主義，[2] 而消費與擬像之間的交互作用，則是使幻想工程持續運轉的主要動力元件。小至修圖與濾鏡的照騙、大至社會上的一切購買，都是擬像與消費在當代最誘人的系統。與「成為更好的自己」相比，「成為其他」更加迷人。

且讓我們先放下那些將「擬像」觀念偷樑換柱的廉價式道德批判與憂鬱犬儒之姿，在由王韓芳策展的「主題樂園幻想工程挑戰賽」（簡稱「幻想工程」展）中觀看作為超真實的擬像消費。「幻想工程」展集結了跨不同世代的敘事者，他們大多透過動態影像和裝置來構築情境與敘事。其複合媒材與碎片化是拒絕敘事單點透視的方法，是藝術家在思考有別於文化工業帝國的新敘事主義方法時的物質面。此種新敘事主義與擴延電影、散文電影共處在一個沒有血緣關係的變裝家族（drag house）。影像是擬像的介面，而是影像背後的敘事，才是成就擬像的意義系統。

因應台北當代藝術館舉辦前身作為國小學校建築的教室空間結構，「幻想工程」展的每一件作品在不同的單一空間中，有不少作品以情境鮮明的裝置，

文／陳晞

加強自作品外溢的氛圍。何采柔的《假設》（IF）與展覽主視覺開宗明義地在二樓入口處，成為這趟幻想工程參訪之旅的兔子洞。紅底白字的雜誌圖標「IF」修改自美國的經典生活雜誌《LIFE》，然而卻更使我聯想到《IF》雜誌——這本 1952 年出版的科幻雜誌。儘管它並不有名，卻仍是反映戰後現代科技發展的文本，也與策展論述提到的迪士尼樂園誕生於相近的時代。在這層意義上，何采柔的《假設》，即產生了自現實生活抽取幻想敘事的圖示意義，投映在紙本雜誌上的影像，則成為「幻想工程」裡敘事圖像疊加關係的摘要。

科幻故事的幻想工程剛誕生的時候，總因為其對於未知的腦補想像與陰謀論，而被批判為偽科學與不正經的創作（甚至，不被看做是文學創作）。另一方面，迪士尼公司依照美國社會環境而改編的許多故事，則因為它寓教於樂的教化作用[3]而大受家庭喜愛。這不由得讓我想起班雅明提醒我們的事情：說故事是一種人類相互交換經驗、具指點知識與智慧功能的、指導著人們如何過活的一種能力。如今說故事的人成為文化工業的帝國巨頭，它們是一切幻想工程的承包商，是代替親人對我們說故事的人。它們是迪士尼，是 NETFLIX、是 Amazon、是吉卜力、是 YouTuber，這亦是另一件作品《幕後的》以輕盈緩慢的動作，在展場空間規劃中的通道裡，成為對於觀看幻想工程之介面的提示：這是「挑戰賽」，不是幻想工程落成發表會。這裡充滿故事，但不要只成為看故事的人，去看故事怎麼被說的、被哪些人說、用什麼語言、又有什麼樣的敘事結構。

● 另類現代與新敘事

琳賽・席爾在此次展出的作品《雙生纏結[4]（第四劇院）》裡，延用了其經典作品《命運本該如此》（2009）中的双球體投影法，以此將這含有自傳性質的影像，不完整地、分裂式被陳述。她曾在談論《命運本該如此》時表示，她認為不完整更接近真正的生命經驗。[4] 而以不完整來開拓敘事過於絕對的局限，並且讓觀者不只作為一位接收的窺視者，在影像研究者江凌青對於席爾的研究中，她認為席爾的作品呼應了麥可・紐曼（Michael Newman）的影像美學：電影並非只是平面的螢幕，而是具有景深的空間，「裝置形式使得觀者對影像的沉思，與即時的身體經驗，得以同時發生」。[5] 在張允菡的《美國夢》裡，她則是將敘事身份「外包」給插畫師、魔術師與說書人，並且在展場蓋起了一個只能從外面窺探的小屋，讓小屋成為影像與敘事的載體，讓觀者的視線遊覽於小屋內外。在張紋瑄的《腹語術士》和《裝備秀》裡，更揭露了此種詮釋敘事和語言在交互主體性之間的裝置方法。她以揭露領袖強人與成功人士的講演身體著稱，在此次展出的作品中，亦探索了配音員身體技術的探究過程。相映於此命題的科斯塔・托尼夫《人偶》，則以架空敘事的腦補為觀眾說書，說著革命偉人在一個如涅槃般的空無環境裡談論革命。

主題樂園之所以不同於遊樂園，在於敘事在幻想工程裡的形塑場域的方法。它讓你選擇想成為的角色，加入某個敘事裡，與鮮活的角色與場景對話，它是擬像消費在如今的數位時代無處不在的魔幻力量。誰會知道，如今連主題樂園都遭受到數位介面的考驗？特別是歷經 COVID-19 疫情時代的人們，已經逐漸對數位的身體有更講究、更沉浸式的體驗。因此，如果說藝術家是幻

想工程挑戰賽的參賽者，那他們挑戰的，便是如何拒絕那已然文化工業化的故事方法論，重拾自 20 世紀戰後視覺藝術逐漸拋棄的敘事能力。

故事的言說方法、使用的語言系統，與它所隱含的寓言意圖，是幻想工程最核心的材料。工程並不全是靠那些現代工業的硬體物質造就的，儘管在埃里卡・貝克曼（Ericka Beckman）的《轉換中心》，那些影片裡的勞工在一個生硬的工業機房裡，重複操作栓手輪以維持系統運作，旋轉動態的意向在此次她展出的兩件作品裡，看似是以迴圈的勞動所產生的剩餘價值，但是在影片裡突襲幾秒鐘影像的寶可夢特效，卻又推翻了這樣的論點。而且，顏色吸引著我，不論是在工廠環境，還是那在《中斷》裡鮮明的色彩，物質性仍舊是表現張力的所在。這些視覺、裝置與形式一再地提醒我們「動態影像」（Moving Image）與「錄像藝術」（video art）在敘事意圖在本質上的差異。

自 2009 年開始，有越來越多的當代藝術家與策展人，逐漸重拾藝術的圖像與敘事能力。例如尼可拉・布西歐（Nicolas Bourriaud）在關係美學之後提出的「Altermodern」，他將這個概念視為後現代主義的繼任者，認為其反映的，是當前的藝術作為一種探索文本和圖像、時間與空間相互交織的紐帶。他亦以泰特三年展（Altermodern: Tate Triennial 2009）作為展示此一概念的框架；無獨有偶，大都會藝術博物館則舉辦了圍繞在美國加州藝術學院（CalArts）、廳牆藝術中心（Hallwalls）和非營利畫廊組織「藝術家空間」（Artists Space）等三個藝術社群之間的聯展「圖像世代：1974-1984」，旨在探討低限主義之後、以大眾媒體文化、圖片與圖標為創作對象的視覺藝術家。參展「幻想工程」的席爾與貝克曼，皆是上述兩檔重要展覽的參展藝術家，這使展覽有著對新敘事在動態影像裝置實踐中的當代影像美學，有著連結與對話的企圖，並且在這樣的 OTT（over the top）平台時代裡，創發另類的敘事方法。真正能讓我們在展場裡進入敘事的，不是大放厥詞的「男言之癮（mansplaining，或稱為男性說教）」（這檔展覽的參展藝術家性別以女性為主，而多使用非單一的敘事方法），而是充滿孔洞的、多軌的、交互的、不完整的記憶。讓觀者因此被引誘，深入其中成為未知的其他角色，而不只是被動接收的窺探者或學生。

¹ 劍湖山、六福村與九族文化村是台灣三大本地主題樂園。

² 《物體系》，頁 335-342。

³ 例如，有法官會判處犯法的獵鹿人，每個月都必須看《小鹿斑比》。該部片自 1947 年以來多次重新上映，並且在不同時代都影響動保環境的發展。

⁴ 江凌青，〈當代影像的命運：從琳賽·席爾的創作觀察當代錄像裝置對電影美學的擴延與回返〉，2011 世安美學論文獎，頁 24。

⁵ 同上註，頁 24-25。

Entering Stories, Becoming Others: Installations of Moving Images and the Practice of New Narrativism in *Making Worlds: An Imagineering Project*

To undeniably convey the sensory experience of a "journey" to the spectator, a story cannot be rendered too complete and absolute so much so that the spectator can only remain a simple voyeur. The journey must be completed and experienced by the spectator himself. Without the body as a medium, it will not be possible for the tactile space to become more deepened and extended.

—Chiang Ling-Ching, "The Fate of Contemporary Image: Expansion and Revisiting of Film Aesthetics in Contemporary Video Installations in the Work of Lindsay Seers" (2011)

● Becoming Others

For those born in the 90s, the days of compulsory education would surely entail a graduation package tour to the local theme parks of "Shan-Liu-Jiu." [1] As theme parks often require large lots of land, they are usually located in rural areas far away from cities—as castles of entertainment leading to alternative realities for people, amusement facilities are produced with complicated hardware structures to create all sorts of physical excitement, and attract groups of tourists and families for experiences. However, no matter how attractive they have been, they are no match to the enchanting Disneyland or Universal Studios, which are carriers of multiple ways to experience multiple narratives, with magical and fascinating stories.

In the TV series *Westworld*, the character Dr. Ford played by Anthony Hopkins provides us an explanation as to why theme parks as simulacra are so enchanting:

They [consumers] come back because of the subtleties, the details. They come back because they discover something they imagine no one has ever noticed before, something they fall in love with. They're not looking for a story that tells them who they are - they already know who they are. They're here because they want a glimpse of who they could be.

This passage points out Baudrillard's thinking when discussing simulacrum and consumption: from the perspective of *The System of Objects* (*Le Système des Objets*), consumption is not a materialistic practice nor a phenomenology of "abundance" (or excess). Consumption is different from purchasing, possessing, spending and enjoying. The point is not about the clothes, food, or automobiles we buy, but lies in organizing all these elements into signifying entities. Consumption is a virtual whole, a systematized manipulation of signs. Objects are signs that allow consumers to individualize or produce differences. Baudrillard understands consumption as a never-satisfying lack, a purely idealist action. To restrain or regulate it would be naïve or absurd moralism,[2] and the interplay of consumption and simulacrum is the primary propelling component that keeps imagineering projects running. From as small as retouched and filtered pictures of deception to as large as every purchase in society, they are the most alluring systems of the simulacrum and consumption. Comparing to "becoming a better self," it is more appealing to "become others."

By Chen Hsi

Let us temporarily put aside those cheap moral judgments and gloomy cynicism, which intend to replace the concept of "simulacrum" with something that is incorrect, and take a look at the consumption of hyperreal simulacra in *Making Worlds: An Imagineering Project* (referred to as *An Imagineering Project* below) curated by Wang Han-Fang. *An Imagineering Project* brings together artists, or narrative creators in this case, from different generations, who mostly use moving images and installations to construct situations and narratives. Their use of mixed media and fragmentation constitutes the approach to refuse the singular perspective of narrative, and manifests the material aspect when the artists contemplate on alternatives to the new narrativism of the empire of cultural industry. Such new narrativism, expanded cinema, and essay film coinhabit in a drag house without any relations whatsoever. Image is the interface of the simulacrum; and it is the narratives behind images that form the simulacral system of signification.

Due to the classroom-style space of the Museum of Contemporary Art, Taipei, which used to be an elementary school in the past, every work featured in *An Imagineering Project* is showcased in a single space, quite a few of which are installations using vivid situations to reinforce the atmosphere overbrimming from the works. Joyce Ho's *IF*, along with the key visual design of the exhibition, is installed at the entrance leading to the second-floor gallery rooms, forming the rabbit hole into this journey of the imagineering project. The magazine's white logo "IF" with a red background is based on the classic American lifestyle magazine *LIFE*. However, I am more inclined to associate it with another magazine, *IF* – a sci-fi magazine first published in 1952. Despite its lack of fame, the latter is a text that reflects the post-war development of modern technology, and was born in the same era as Disneyland mentioned in the curatorial statement. From this perspective, Ho's *IF* carries the iconic meaning of extracting imaginary narratives from real life; and the image projected onto the paper magazine consequently becomes an abstract of overlapping narratives and images in *An Imagineering Project*.

When the imagineering project of sci-fi stories first emerged, it was always criticized as pseudo-science and unserious creation (it was not even viewed as literary creation) due to the imagination and conspiracy theories about the unknown in such stories. On the other hand, many stories from Disney, which were adapted in accordance with the American social milieu, became immensely well-accepted by common households due to their educational nature and effect of indoctrination. Nowadays, storytellers have transformed into the giants in the empire of cultural industry. They are the subcontractors of everything related to imagineering, and have replaced our families to tell us stories—think about Disney, NETFLIX, Amazon, Ghibli, and all the YouTubers. This is also the hint that *Behind the Scene* – another work characterized by gentle, slow movements and serving as an interface to viewing imagineering displayed in the corridor space of the exhibition – attempts to provide: this is a "challenge race" rather than an inaugural presentation of an imagineering project. Here is a place full of stories, but do not just remain a story reader—instead, pay attention to how stories are told, the storytellers, the languages in which the stories are told, and their narrative structures.

● Alternative Modernity and New Narrative

In the exhibition, Lindsay Seers exhibits *Entangled*[4]*(Theatre IV)*, which continues the format of dual spherical projection used in her iconic work, *It Has to Be This Way* (2009), to convey a somewhat autobiographical video in an incomplete, divided manner. When talking about *It Has to Be This Way*, Seers states that being incomplete more closely reflected one's authentic life experiences.[4] Consequently, utilizing incompleteness, she expands the restricting absoluteness of narrative, and renders the spectator not merely a voyeur on the receiving end. In her research about Seers, film researcher Chiang Ling-Ching argues that Seers's work echoes the image aesthetics of Michael Newman: movie is not (just) a flat screen, but a space with depth—"the form of installation enables the spectator's thinking about image and immediate bodily experience to take place at the same time."[5] In Chang Yun-Han's *American Dream*, the artist "outsources" the role of narrator to illustrators, magicians, and storytellers. She builds a small hut in the exhibition space, which can only be glimpsed into from the outside, turning the hut into a vehicle of image and narrative, so the audience's vision can only stay outside the hut. Chang Wen-Hsuan's *The Ventriloquist* and *The Equipment Show* further reveal the installation method to interpret the intersubjectivity between narrative and language. Chang is known for exposing the body of powerful leaders and successful figures in speeches. In her works featured in the exhibition, she also explores the bodily techniques of voice actors. In a similar way, Kosta Tonev's *Dolls* tells stories based on imaginary narratives, and portrays revolutionary figures talking about revolutions in a nirvana-like environment of void.

The difference between theme parks and amusement parks lies in how narrative shapes the site in an imagineering project. It allows you to choose the role you wish to play, participate in a certain narrative, and dialogue with vibrant characters and scenes—this is the omnipresent magical power of simulacral consumption in the digital time. However, who would have known that even theme parks are put to the test by digital interfaces nowadays? Especially, having undergone the COVID-19 pandemic, people have gradually grown accustomed to more particular and immersive experience for the digital body. As a result, if the artists are the participants in this challenging race of the imagineering project, their challenge would be how to refuse the storytelling method of cultural industrialization and retrieve the ability of narrative, which has been gradually abandoned by visual arts after the war in the 20th century.

The approaches of storytelling, the linguistic system used, and the hidden morals of stories are the most crucial materials of an imagineering project, which does not entirely rely on the material hardware of modern industries. Although in Ericka Beckman's *Switch Center*, the laborers in the video are engaging in repetitively operating the wheels to maintain the working of the system in a rigid industrial motor room. The imagery of turning can be found in both works exhibited by Beckman, which appear to signal the surplus value produced by the loop of labor work. However, the sudden special effect of Pokémon popping up for a few seconds in the video seems to overthrow such an argument. Furthermore, the colors are fairly appealing, whether it is in the factory setting or the vibrant colors in *Hiatus*—materiality is still the locus of expressive tension. These visualities, installations, and forms repeatedly remind us that "moving image" and "video art" are essentially different in terms of narrative intention.

Since 2009 onward, more and more contemporary artists and curators have gradually retrieved the image and narrative ability of art. For instance, after his relational aesthetics, Nicolas Bourriaud has put forth the idea of "altermodern," which he sees as the successor to post-modernism, and argues that the altermodern reflects how art at the current stage serves as a bond to explore the interweaving text and image as well as time and space. He further uses *Altermodern: Tate Triennial 2009* as a framework to demonstrate this concept. Coincidentally, the Metropolitan Museum of Art has organized a group exhibition, titled *The Pictures Generation, 1974-1984*, which revolves around three art communities: the CalArts, the Hallwalls, and the non-profit gallery organization, Artists Space. The group exhibition features visual artists who have utilized mass media culture, pictures and icons as their creative subject after minimalism. Both featuring in *An Imagineering Project*, Seers and Beckman have also taken part in the two major exhibitions. This shows that the exhibition does intend to establish a connection and dialogue with the contemporary image aesthetics of the new narrative in the practice of moving-image installations, and create alternative narrative approaches in this era of the over-the-top (OTT) media service. What really enables us to enter the narratives in the exhibition is not the unbashful "mansplaining" (the artists featured in this exhibition are mainly women, most of whom use a non-singular narrative approach) but the porous, multi-channeled, interrelated, incomplete memories, which lure in the spectator into playing unknown roles rather than being a voyeur or a student on the passively receiving end.

---

[1] The three major local theme parks in Taiwan back then were the Janfushan (also spelled as Jianhushan) Theme Park, the Leofoo (also spelled as Liufu) Village Theme Park, and the Formosa Aboriginal Cultural Park (its Mandarin name is literally translated as Jiuzu Cultural Park, referring to the initial nine indigenous peoples in Taiwan).

[2] *The System of Objects*, pp. 335-42.

[3] For instance, judges would sentence hunters who hunt deer illegally to watch *Bambi* every month. Since the film was premiered in 1947, it has been re-screened in cinema many times, and has influenced the development of animal and environmental protection in different eras.

[4] Chiang Ling-Ching, "The Fate of Contemporary Image: Expansion and Revisiting of Film Aesthetics in Contemporary Video Installations in the Work of Lindsay Seers." Recipient of the 2011 S-An Aesthetics Award, p. 24.

[5] *Ibid*. pp. 24-5.

策展人與藝術家簡介 About the Curator and Artists

策展人與藝術家簡介 About the Curato

策展人 ● 王韓芳
CURATOR
● WANG HAN-FANG

王韓芳為獨立藝術文化工作者與策展人，她關注當代生活的表徵，思索相關的生命經驗變化其來何自，並進行相關方向的假說與研究。核心興趣在於思索科技、文明及知識發展如何帶來人的重新定義及人與外在關係的重整，同時也思索技術作為一種社會基礎結構，將如何影響個人的感知經驗、主體性建構及未來的群體生活與社會想像。王韓芳曾獲補助駐地美國紐約 Performa19 雙年展臺灣館 curatorial fellow，也曾以合作者角色（與張恩滿、鄒婷共同合作）參與 documenta 15 展出計畫「漂浮的蝸牛系統：入侵計畫」。近期策劃展覽包含：2021 年「大象奏鳴曲：王雅慧個展」（台東美術館）、2019 年「即溶生活：未來記憶的想像」（MoNTUE 北師美術館）及 2018 年「離線瀏覽」第六屆台灣國際錄像藝術展助理策展人（許家維、許峰瑞雙策展，鳳甲美術館）。

Han-Fang Wang is an independent curator and art worker. In 2019, she received a grant as a resident curatorial fellow for the Taiwan Pavilion at Performa 19 in New York, and in 2022, she collaborated with En-Man Chang and Ting Tsou in the project of *Floating System for Snails: Project Invasion* in documenta fifteen. Her recent curatorial projects include: *Still Life Sonata: Wang Yahui Solo Exhibition*, Taitung Art Museum, Taitung, Taiwan (2021); *Mercurial Boundaries: Imagining Future Memory*, Museum of National Taipei University of Education, Taipei, Taiwan (2019); and *the 6th Taiwan International Video Art Exhibition: Offline Browser* (curated by Hsu Chia-Wei and Hsu Fong-Ray), assistant curator, Hong-Gah Museum, Taipei, Taiwan (2018).

Intrigued by the facade of contemporary life, Wang ponders the changing states of human experiences, and conducts relevant research that tests her hypotheses regarding the direction in which humanity moves. She is profoundly concerned about the ways technology, civilization, and knowledge redefine humanity and its relationship with the world. At the same time, she contemplates how technology, as a form of social infrastructure, plays a role in the individual's perceptual experience, the construction of their subjectivity, as well as life as a collective and as a society in the future.

藝術家 ● 何采柔
ARTIST
● JOYCE HO

何采柔（b.1983，臺灣），加州大學國際關係學士，愛荷華大學藝術研究所碩士。自 2010 年開始嘗試編導工作。無論是以繪畫、裝置或影像的方式創作，何采柔的作品總能以局部分解的動作、日常習慣的切片與豐富迷離的光影，呈現人與現實之間某種既親密又疏離的緊張關係。而這些獨特而強烈的創作一方面包圍著觀眾，卻又與其保持對峙的狀態，讓日常的片刻成為了一道風景或儀式。

Joyce Ho (b.1983, Taiwan) received her M.A. in studio arts from the University of Iowa. She is an interdisciplinary artist, focusing specifically on moving image, installation, and performance. With an illusion rich in light and shadow, the artistic conception aims to integrate the deconstructed movements and fragmented slices of daily routines. As such, the artist endeavors, whether in painting, installation or video, to convey an intimate, yet alienated tensions between human beings and reality. The singularly intensive creation simultaneously captivates and confronts viewers, which almost renders a quotidian moment into a piece of landscape or a ritual.

藝術家 ● 張紋瑄
ARTIST
● CHANG WEN-HSUAN

張紋瑄（b.1991，臺灣）的藝術實踐透過重讀、重寫及虛構出另類方案，來質問機構化歷史的敘事結構，並同時暴露出潛藏在歷史敘事中，不同權力之間的角力關係，而此暴露結構的手段，也正是一種重新處理個人故事及歷史書寫之間的關係及能動性的方式。藉由不同的媒介——包含裝置、錄像及講述——的使用，他經常用與原件有誤差的檔案以及第一人稱敘事，讓觀者得以反思歷史如何影響了當下的形塑與未來的推進。自 2018 年起開啟〈書寫公廠 Writing FACTory〉長期計畫。

The artistic practice of Chang Wen-Hsuan (b.1991, Taiwan) questions the narrative structure of institutionalised history with re-readings, re-writing, and suggestions of fictional alternatives. To expose the power tensions embedded in historical narratives is a way of managing the relationships and dynamics between individual stories and the writing of history. Through versatile platforms including installations, videos, and lectures, she often navigates skewed documentations and first-person accounts to trigger reflections on how the understanding of history affects the purport of the present and thrust of the future. In 2018, she launched the project *Writing FACTory*.

藝術家 ● 琳賽・席爾
ARTIST
● LINDSAY SEERS

琳賽・席爾工作於倫敦，居住於謝佩島（Isle of Sheppey）。席爾以其行為表演、錄像裝置及他以自己身體做為攝影機所創作的許多影像作品為人所知。席爾的創作以各種省略性的敘事方法（elliptical narratives）探索複雜的概念和情境，因為在他的想法中，各種行動將會誘發連續變化的諸多關聯事件與巧合，而這將導致一種複雜且糾纏的狀態。席爾的研究關注意識本質，並深受哲學家亨利・柏格森（Henri Bergson）及神經科學家克里斯・弗里斯（Chris Frith）和阿尼爾・賽斯（Anil Seth）的影響。藝術家本人被診斷有自閉症及神經多樣性的特質，而這也反映在其具大量重複性和複雜性的作品上。

Lindsay Seers works in London and lives on the Isle of Sheppey. She is best known for her performances, video installations and the hundreds of images she has produced using her own body as a camera. Her works explore complex ideas and situations through elliptical narratives that are shaped by an evolving set of connections and coincidences that the act of making evokes. Concerned with the nature of consciousness, Seers' research is influenced profoundly by the philosopher Henri Bergson and the neuroscientists Chris Frith and Anil Seth. Seers is diagnosed with autism and neurodiverse. This reflects in her art works which shows an excess of multiplicity and complexity.

藝術家 ● 科斯塔·托尼夫
ARTIST
● KOSTA TONEV

科斯塔·托尼夫（b.1980，保加利亞）是工作並居住於奧地利維也納的視覺藝術家。他畢業於保加利亞索菲亞國立藝術學院（National Academy of Art in Sofia），並取得奧地利維也納美術學院（Academy of Fine Arts in Vienna）碩士學位。托尼夫的創作不侷限於其原初的繪畫背景，他發展出以文本為基礎，具表演性（performative），且結合攝影、錄像、裝置及聲音等媒材的創作。他探索藝術式研究的領域，並對語言及敘事方法有高度興趣。在他的作品中，他所建構的敘事多涉及音樂、電影、思想論述和流行文化，運用現實生活經驗或虛構的第二自我（alter ego），以幽默、戲謔的方式探討歷史及政治的相關議題，並藉此延伸出第一人稱觀點的當下考古。

Kosta Tonev (b. 1980, Bulgaria) is a visual artist based in Vienna, Austria. He received a BA degree from the National Academy of Art in Sofia and an MA degree from the Academy of Fine Arts in Vienna. In the years that followed, his work expanded beyond his initial training as a painter to include performative and text-based approaches, employing the media of photography, video, installation and sound. His interests in language and storytelling are closely linked to the field of artistic research. He constructs narratives involving references to music, film, intellectual discourse, and popular culture. Drawing on his own experiences or an alter ego he has invented, he often addresses issues around history and politics in a humorous and playful way. In the process, the artist renders a complex archaeology of the present, told in the first person.

藝術家 ● 埃里卡·貝克曼
ARTIST
● ERICKA BECKMAN

埃里卡·貝克曼（b.1951，紐約）是圖像世代（Pictures Generation）的關鍵藝術家之一。他的作品探索了在大眾傳播的年代，個人自我意象的塑造如何受到外部意見影響。他的影像和裝置常藉由顏色、聲音及動作去檢視文化符號及主體性，並特別聚焦於勞動、娛樂及性別議題。自 1970 年代中期以來，在電影、錄像、裝置和攝影創作中，貝克曼打造了一種標誌性的視覺語彙。他的影像趣味詼諧並帶有批判性，取藉各種遊戲與童話故事的結構與運作機制，融合創造出外於現存的運行規則，同時也觸及他者與身分、權力與控制等深刻的問題探討。

Ericka Beckman (b. 1951, New York) is considered a key figure of the Pictures Generation, whose work investigates how individuals shape their self-image based on outside influencers during an age of mass media. The moving image works and installations created by her use of color, sound, and movement to examine cultural signs and subjectivity, particularly with regard to labor, leisure and gender. Since the mid-1970s, Beckman has forged a signature visual language in film, video, installation, and photography. Her creations are playfully satirical and critical at the same time, and by incorporating various structural elements and the logics of games and fairytales, she has established unconventional structures and rules, while also profoundly exploring issues on topics such as others and identity, as well as power and control.

藝術家 ● 張允菡
ARTIST
● CHANG YUN–HAN

張允菡（b.1985，臺灣）大學及研究所主修雕塑，習慣移動，容易分心，經常被不重要的小事吸引，認為幽默是重要的事情。她的作品多源於對身處環境的觀察與思考，喜歡在不同環境的變動中保持靈活，探尋事物被建構、理解的各種方式。透過觀察社會集體的各種樣貌，並運用創作轉換成為不同媒材與形式的呈現，希望在個人觀點與他人的共感經驗間找到微妙的平衡。近期創作多從文字開始發展，但於正式展覽前都不確定最後的會是什麼。

Chang Yun Han's (b.1985, Taiwan) art practice focuses on the subtle invisibilities in everyday life. Through her observation in different cities or societies, she explores those common but differentiated experiences between individuals and collectives that were waiting to be named. Her creation tries to examine how these differentiations are constructed, and she rephrases those stories through different mediums and methods. She believes that art lives in reality, and through imagination human beings could create potential breaches to broaden perception.

圖錄 Plates 圖錄 Plates 圖錄 Plates 圖錄 Plates 圖錄 Plates 圖錄 Plates 圖錄 Plates 圖錄 Plates 圖錄 Plates 圖錄 Pla
圖錄 Plates 圖錄 Plates 圖錄 Plates 圖錄 Plates 圖錄 Plates 圖錄 Plates 圖錄 Plates 圖錄 Plates

何采柔
JOYCE HO

《假設》
IF

1964 年於紐約的世界博覽會，華特·迪士尼受邀為奇異公司、百事可樂及福特汽車發展裝置，爾後這些裝置被轉移至佛羅里達州，成為了第一個迪士尼樂園中的特點設施。在那個年代的世界博覽會，除了有國家競爭的意圖，同時也帶著科技展示及美好的未來生活想像。奇異公司展區「進步之城」中展出了象徵進步的旋轉木馬（Carousel of Progress），這個劇場式的裝置，以旋轉的圓形舞臺為中心，四周環繞著觀眾席。舞臺上演示著各年代家庭生活場景，述說電力系統的發展進程及其在每個年代生活中所扮演的角色。

作品《假設》（IF），一本以「LIFE」為名的新聞攝影周刊封面，畫面捕捉激情的群眾會聚在賽事廣場中。藝術家透過影像將「LIFE」轉化為「IF」，並將賽事廣場上安置了原先並不存在的旋轉木馬。荒謬的情境對比周遭激昂圍觀的群眾，不斷旋轉的木馬加上標題 IF 與 LIFE 之間的耐人尋味，創造出交會於進步、競爭與群眾欲望之間的想像空間。

The 1964 New York World's Fair featured exhibits produced by Walt Disney for General Electric, Pepsi-Cola, and Ford, which were later transferred to Florida and went on to become the first Disney Park attractions. The World's Fair at the time was considered a competition between countries, and at the same time, it was also a place to showcase technology and wonderful visions for life in the future. Inside the exhibit space, "Progressland", sponsored by the General Electric Company, was the "Carousel of Progress". A symbol of advancement, this theatrical installation had a rotating circular stage in the center and was enclosed by the audience on all sides. Displayed on the stage were scenes from everyday home life in the 1900s, 1920s, 1940s and 21st century, which showcased the advancement of the electric power system and its role in people's lives throughout different eras.

The artwork *IF* presents a cover of the photojournalism magazine, *LIFE*. It shows a lively crowd congregated on a sports arena. The artist visually transforms "LIFE" into "IF" and places a previously nonexistent carousel on the square. An interesting and absurd juxtaposition is formed with the rowdy onlookers and the incessantly rotating carousel with signs of "IF" and "LIFE" shown. An imaginary space is created with intertwining elements of progress, competition, and the desire of the masses.

二樓西側樓梯／Western Stairway 2F
投影於繪畫過的雜誌封面｜雜誌含框：34.5 x 25.5 x 1.2 cm｜2017 年
Projection on painted magazine cover｜Magazine with frame：34.5 x 25.5 x 1.2 cm｜2017

琳賽・席爾
LINDSAY SEERS

《雙生纏結[4]（第四劇院）》
Entangled[4] (Theatre IV)

作品《雙生纏結[4]（第四劇院）》擬將展間化為劇院，以兩個觀看席、一齣演出及兩個圓洞式觀景窗等空間形式，將兩位觀眾分別帶入兩則高度關聯的影像。在整件作品中，雙生的狀態將穿越形式、內容及圖像不斷地交錯出現，如：在性別方面，以維多利亞時期女扮男裝的劇場演員海蒂・金（Hetty King）及維斯塔・緹莉（Vesta Tilley）作為主角；而在過去與當下之間，則以現下的演員演繹過去的角色；在自我與外在間，藝術家與主角互為關係；在形式上，球體則同時是眼球、迪斯可球亦是海灘球。觀眾將同時處於看與被看的狀態，所有敘事及其意涵在此空間中被拆分成片段並混合，隱喻一種相互聯繫、同時並存的現實、時間和意識概念，也藉此展開故事在不同脈絡下的多重性。

在此展中，此作猶似一個引言情境，揭示著敘事於此開始不斷分裂、變形、複製與成長，直至個人／集體、真實／虛構、形式與內容之間的界線不復存在，形成一個近似海洋的漂浮狀態。

Entangled[4] (Theatre IV) transforms the exhibition room into a theater, with two audience seats, a performance, and two circular viewing windows, transporting two viewers respectively into two interrelated videos. In the whole work, the entangled state continues to appear intermittently in terms of form, content and image: Gender-wise, Hetty King and Vesta Tilley, two Victorian male impersonators are the main characters in this work. The past and the present become entangled as modern actors interpret historical roles. The entanglement between the self and the external world is shown through the interrelation between the artist and the protagonists. With regards to the form, the spherical shape indicates simultaneously eyeballs, disco balls and beach balls. The audience are both watching and being watched. Therefore, in this space, all narratives and their implications are deconstructed into segments and mixed together, serving as a metaphor for interconnecting, coexisting reality, time, and consciousness, while the multiplicity of the story in a different context is unfurled.

In this exhibition, this work serves as a preface, from which the narrative starts to split, morph, reproduce, and grow until the boundaries between the individual/the collective, the real/the fictional, the form/the content gradually disappear, forming a precarious state as if everything seems to be floating on the sea.

205 展間／R205

雙頻道錄像裝置｜尺寸依場地而定｜2022 年
Dual screen installation｜Dimensions variable｜2022

● 圖片提供：琳賽・席爾 *Entangled[2] (Theatre II)*, 2013 (production still). Courtesy of the artist and Matt's Gallery, London.
● Photo credit: Lindsay Seers, *Entangled[2] (Theatre II)*, 2013 (production still). Courtesy of the artist and Matt's Gallery, London.

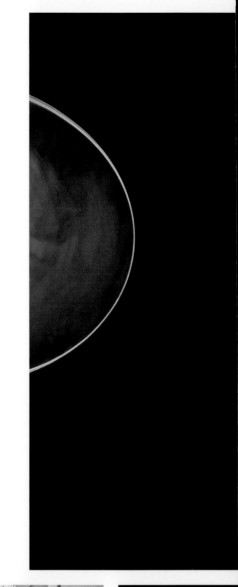

因为往外看就好像得光被分裂一样
So looking out it as if it's being split.

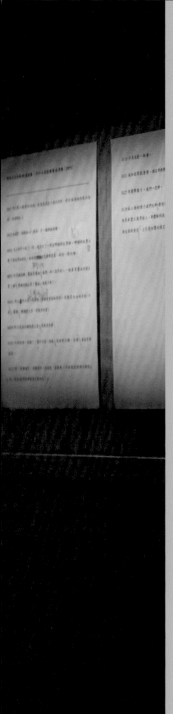

張紋瑄
CHANG WEN-HSUAN

《腹語術士》
The Ventriloquist

敘事是體驗的核心,一個好的講故事方式,有機會建構或操縱各種世界觀。自 20 世紀開始,許多敘事的討論由時間轉向至空間:從連續性至同在性,從線性文字至聲音圖像,從物理空間、大眾傳媒至虛擬現實。跨媒介的空間敘事需要填充更多的場景描繪與表演擬真式的技巧,好讓觀眾進入被建立的敘事空間,通過媒介經驗的行為成為一種媒介事件,也形成一種替代真實,以致觀眾能投入「表演」,同時也成為敘事中的角色之一。如同,見證時任行政院長的蔣經國在發表十大建設演講時的激昂與嚴厲,以及見證李光耀於 1965 年新馬分裂後在記者面前的啜泣與堅持。在他們的演說中,聲音除了推進敘事,聲音表情也同時傳達了說話者的人設、身處空間、與接受者的設定關係等。作品《腹語術士》將這些敘事的結構拆開,以配音技術及腹語術作為敘事技術——聲音的探勘主軸,除了攤開展示並分析聲音扮演的角色,也於表現形式中思考「說」與「秀」的技術。

At the core of an experience is a narrative, and good story-telling has the potential to construct or manipulate different ways of seeing the world. Since the 20th century, many discussions on narrative have shifted their focus from temporality to spatiality, going from continuity to being present, from linear text to audiovisual, and from physical space, mass media to virtual reality. Transdisciplinary spatial narratives require the use of techniques that can lead to more depictions of scenes and performances of realistic simulation, which would immerse the audience in a constructed narrative space. A mediated event then manifests from the acts of mediated experience and subsequently becomes a substitute for reality. Members of the audience are able to get involved in the "performance" and also become one of the characters in the story. Just like witnessing the passionate and forceful speech on the nation's "Ten Major Construction Projects" given by Chiang Ching-Kuo, the then President of the Executive Yuan of the Republic of China, and the press conference speech given by Lee Kuan Yew in 1965 when Singapore separated from Malaysia and became independent, their speeches were not just about vocally pushing forward the narratives, but their vocal expressions also conveyed the speakers' public persona, the spaces they were in, and the designated relationships formed with their recipients. *The Ventriloquist* deconstructs the structures of these narratives and uses techniques of dubbing and ventriloquism for storytelling, and with focus placed on exploring voices, in addition to openly showcasing and analyzing the role of voice, the techniques of "speaking" and "putting on a show" are also examined through expressive formats.

204展間╱R204

單頻道錄像裝置、文件｜尺寸依場地而定｜2021 年
Single-channel video installation, documents｜Dimensions variable｜2021

導演:張紋瑄／剪輯:張紋瑄／聲音演員:李香生、林芳雪／
攝影:李益丞、林詠翌／後製:萬事屋影像制作／翻譯:王怡文

Director: Chang Wen-Hsuan / Editing: Chang Wen-Hsuan /
Voice actor: Li Xiang-Sheng, Lin Fang-Xue / Cinematography: Lee Yi-Cheng, Lin Yong-Yi /
Post-Production: Onez Production / Translator: Yvonne Kennedy

科斯塔・托尼夫
KOSTA TONEV

《人偶》（第 1 集）、《人偶》（第 2 集）
Dolls (I) and *Dolls (II)*

作品《人偶》（第 1 集、第 2 集）藉由一場來世的超現實相遇，讓數個具有影響力的公眾人物於身後化作另一種存在形式復活。他們成為市場上被大量製造的公仔，於商品化的生命與世界中，他們的肖像被挪用與化約，他們的思想著作被轉化為符號物件，而其生平則成為可被編纂言說的傳奇故事。人物之間以戲謔的對談方式探討著前世今生，質問商品化的各種形式及其效應。然而，似乎在這個經濟遊戲系統中，任何人也無法脫離被賦予的角色。藝術家以隱含革命色彩的人物，如：切・格瓦拉（Che Guevara）、毛澤東、芙烈達・卡蘿（Frida Kahlo）及約瑟夫・史達林（Joseph Stalin）等，在權力失去了地理與疆界的世界中，探討革命的不可能。

Dolls (I) and *Dolls (II)* enact a surreal encounter in the afterlife, and bring several influential public figures back to life in an alternative form after death—that is, as mass produced action figure merchandise sold in the market. In this commodified life and world, their portraits are appropriated and reduced, their ideas and publications transformed into symbolic objects, and their life stories written as legends and tales edited and circulated. In the series, these figures talk about their previous and new lives in a humor and sarcastic way, while questioning various forms of commodification and their effects. However, it seems that none of them could ever be free from the roles they have been given in this systemic game of economy. With revolutionary figures, such as Che Guevara, Mao Zedong, Frida Kahlo, Joseph Stalin, etc., the artist addresses the impossibility of revolution in a world where power has no territory nor boundary.

203 展間／R203

《人偶》（第 1 集）*Dolls (I)*
單頻道錄像裝置｜15 分鐘｜2020 年
Single-channel video installation｜15 min.｜2020

● 圖片提供：科斯塔・托尼夫｜© Bildrecht, Vienna, 2020
● Photo credit: Kosta Tonev｜© Bildrecht, Vienna, 2020

《人偶》（第 2 集）*Dolls (II)*
單頻道錄像裝置｜17 分鐘｜2022 年
Single-channel video installation｜17 min.｜2022

● 圖片提供：科斯塔・托尼夫｜© Bildrecht, Vienna, 2022
● Photo credit: Kosta Tonev｜© Bildrecht, Vienna, 2022
● 創作贊助：The Austrian Federal Ministry for Arts, Culture, Civil Service and Sport.
● The work was funded by the Austrian Federal Ministry for Arts, Culture, Civil Service and Sport.

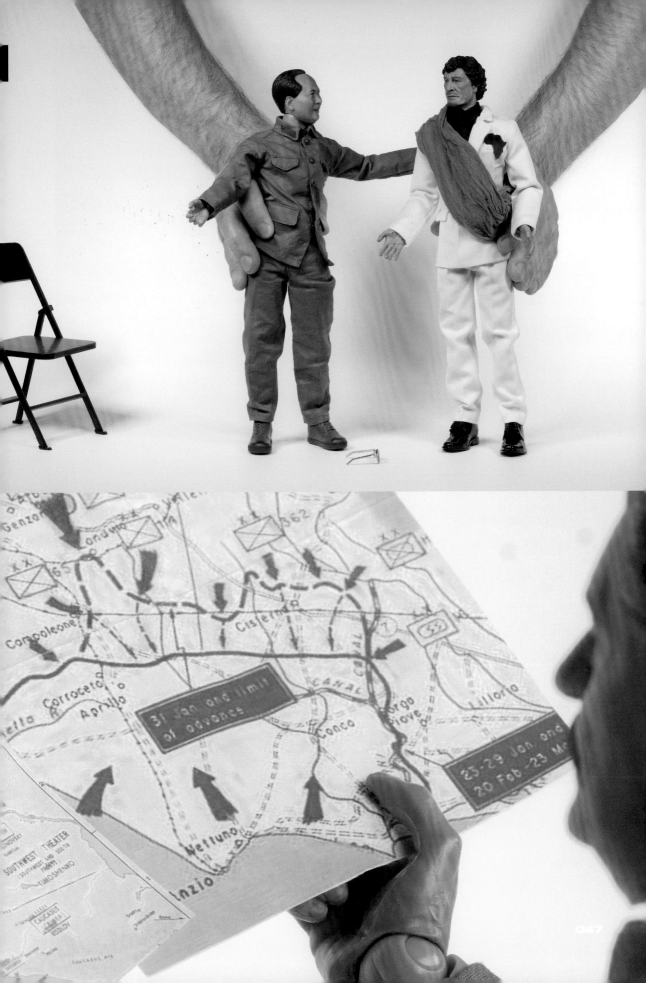

張紋瑄
CHANG WEN-HSUAN

《裝備秀》
The Equipment Show

在時間敘事中，我們會將視點放在故事的連續性上；而在空間敘事中，則會藉由場景空間的描繪將觀眾視線與經驗聚焦於與空間同在。藉由場景的堆疊，接受者將會更加注意角色的眼神、表情、手勢、走位及衣著等，並理解感受其為一種非語言的敘事線，更甚是一種可供辨認的符號指涉。《裝備秀》蒐羅 YouTube 上的影像紀錄，從歷史人物、政治人物、電影角色到成功學講師等，通過他們以肢體動作進行溝通並操作權力為範例，同場邀請劇場演員進行動作拆解並拍攝教學帶，由藝術家扮演的成功學講師 Victoria Chang 亦將講評反饋這些身體與行為技巧，進行分析其與文本及影像之間的結構關係。

In a temporal narrative, we tend to focus on the story's continuity. However, in a spatial narrative, the audience's visual experience and perception become focused on the sense of "presence" through the depiction of scenes. Through the mise-en-scènes, the recipients would begin to pay more attention to the characters' gazes, facial expressions, gestures, movements, and clothing, and they can then comprehend that what they are experiencing is a non-verbal narrative line, or even a recognizable symbolic reference. *The Equipment Show* collects videos uploaded on YouTube, including clips of historical figures, politicians, movie characters, and motivational speakers. Their physical gestures are then presented as examples of communication and power manipulation, with stage performers invited to deconstruct those gestures and also make a tutorial video. The artist plays the role of Victoria Chang, a motivational speaker, who gives feedback on their physical and behavioral skills and analyzes the structural relationships they hold with the texts and the images.

202展間／R202

六頻道錄像裝置｜彩色，無聲，循環播放｜單頻道錄像｜彩色，雙聲道｜2021-2022 年
Six-channel video installation｜Color, silent, loop｜Single-channel video｜Color, stereo｜2021-2022

導演：張紋瑄／剪輯：張紋瑄／動作設計及演出：賀湘儀／攝影：李益丞、林詠翌／後製：萬事屋影像制作
Director: Chang Wen-Hsuan / Editing: Chang Wen-Hsuan / Choreography and Performance: Ho Hsiang-Yi / Cinematography: Lee Yi-Cheng, Lin Yong-Yi / Post-Production: Onez Production

埃里卡・貝克曼
ERICKA BECKMAN

《上框》
Frame UP

《上框》以紐約沃克藝術中心（Walker Art Center）的建築工地作為拍攝場景，並將都市建設的景觀轉換為帶著遊戲性質的巨大彈珠檯。城市內的建築工地本身，即是載寓了都市發展和種種欲望投射的空間，它們既是製造世界的縮影，也可視為人類活動的劇場。藝術家將建築工地內機具物件的位置、造形以及佈局，加上工人們勞動中的身體運動，以雙頻道影像開啟一場彈珠檯遊戲。城市工地成為彈珠檯的視覺與背景故事，但似乎無論是哪一個彈珠檯，雖然城市背景的樣貌及其結構不一定雷同，但彈珠的彈跳、反射抑或得分的機制卻頗為相似。

Frame UP was filmed at a construction site of New York's Walker Art Center and transformed the urban development landscape into a vast pinball game. Building sites in cities are embodiments of urban development and appear to be spaces for the projections of desire – they're microcosms of world-building and can also be seen as theaters of human activities. The construction site became the pinball "backglass" for this dual screen film created by the artist, incorporating the placements, shapes, and arrangements of machines and tools and the movements of the workers' laborious bodies. Considering the visual aspects and the background story involved with transforming an urban construction site into a pinball game, despite the dissimilarities between the backgrounds and structures of individual cities, some similarities still exist between them, just as the ways that pinballs are hit, knocked around, and put into slots to score are the same, even though different pinball arcade games may have different themes.

二樓中樓梯／Central Stairway 2F

雙頻道錄像、多格式影像轉數位檔案｜彩色，有聲｜8 分鐘循環播放｜2005 年
Dual screen, multiple capture formats｜transferred to digital file｜Color, sound｜8 min. loop｜2005

● 圖片提供：埃里卡・貝克曼
● Photo credit: Ericka Beckman

埃里卡・貝克曼
ERICKA BECKMAN

《轉換中心》
Switch Center

《轉換中心》以布達佩斯近郊一座前蘇維埃時期遺留下來的淨水廠作為拍攝場景，在作品中，藝術家摒除言說的敘事，以畫面使用的顏色、聲音及演員動作驅動影像，並透過快速的組接，形成一種視覺上的舞作與音樂。其中，演員身著連身工作服，推轉輪盤、按下鈕鍵抑或移動管線，這些近似機械化的身體動作，轉化為帶著表演性的聲響。藝術家曾表示，這類型的蘇維埃現代化建築，完全體現建造的目的，亦完美地符合其信仰的意識型態，透過在建築物內工作的勞動力操作，鮮明地體現未來實用主義的形式結構。

Switch Center was shot in an abandoned water purification plant from the Soviet era located on the outskirts of Budapest. Forging a verbal narrative, the artist opted to use color, sound, and the performers' movements to activate the film, forming a visual choreography and musical composition through a montage of energetic pacing. Performers are seen dressed in overalls and are either turning a wheel, pushing on buttons, or handling pipelines, with their machine-like physical movements transformed into sounds of performative quality. According to the artist, the Soviet's Modernist Architecture embodied perfectly not only their purpose, but also the ideology upon which they were built. The structure itself comes to life through the movements of the workers inside the building, with a tribute made to futuristic architecture.

201 展間／R201

單頻道錄像裝置、16 釐米膠卷轉 HD｜彩色，有聲｜12 分鐘｜2003 年
Single screen installation, 16mm transferred to HD file｜Color, sound｜12 min.｜2003

● 圖片提供：埃里卡・貝克曼
● Photo credit: Ericka Beckman

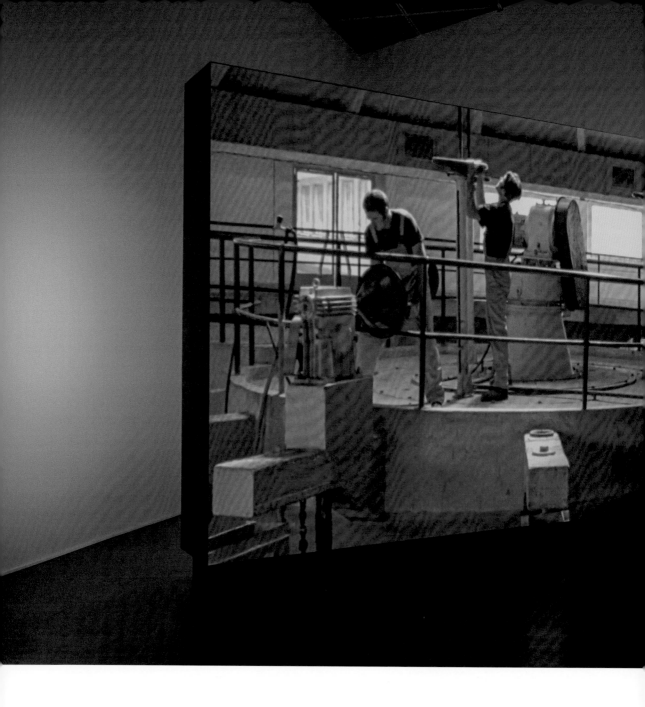

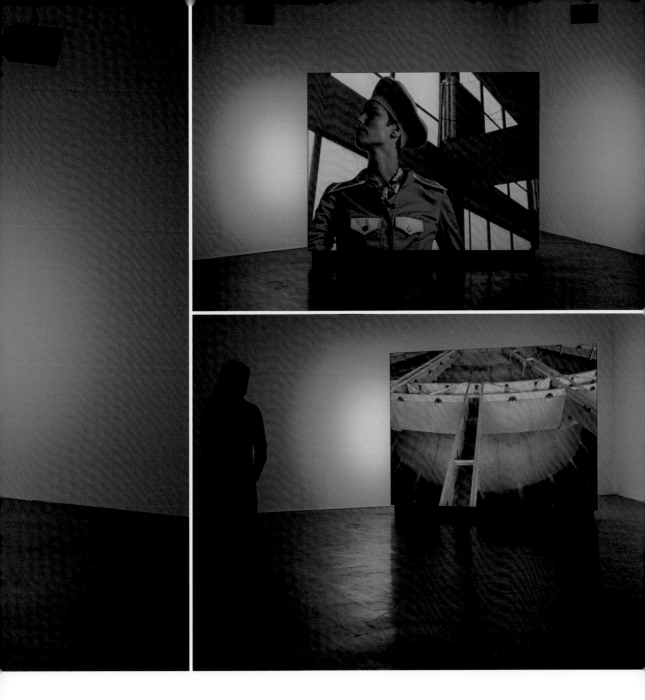

何采柔
JOYCE HO

《幕後的》
Behind the Scene

一道尋常的居家空間中的毛玻璃拉門，門後一位動作標準、情緒中性的真人人偶，以毛玻璃拉門作為「幕」的一種形式，往復地向左及向右推拉，而幕後的影像則隨著幕的運動，產生暫留、變形與組合等微妙的視覺差異。「幕」可以化做各種形式的演出——生活、臺前——臺後、演員——觀眾的界線，門前的世界，觀眾的視線通過「幕」觀看，巨觀上相似的身體，而微觀上視覺組成的改變；門後的世界，真人人偶與看不見的操偶師彼此相互代表，藉由「幕」感受自身的倒影與幕前演示的一個（多個）身體疊合與位移。在幕前幕後間，創作者通過主觀心智來想像並感知集體性，而觀者則通過物質化且半透明的幕，觀看幕的運動與機制，並行創造幕後的分眾世界。

Behind an ordinary fuzzy glass pull door is a human puppet with routine gestures and neutral emotion. The fuzzy glass pull door serves as a curtain, or a scene, and is repeatedly pushed and pulled to the left and right. The movements result in intricate optical illusions caused by vision persistence, distortion, and various combinations. This "curtain" can be transformed into various formats of performance/everyday life, frontstage/backstage, and also serves as the line between the performer and audience. At the world in front of the door, the gaze of the audience passes through the "curtain" and sees a body that remains largely the same but goes through intricate combinations of visual changes. At the world behind the door, a mutual representation exists between the human puppet and the invisible puppeteer, and self-reflection and the singular (or plural) overlapping and displacing body (bodies) displayed in front of the scene are sensed via this "curtain". Dealing with both in front of and behind the scene, the artist subjectively imagines and perceives a sense of collectiveness. On the other hand, through the material and semi-transparent curtain, the audience sees the movements and the mechanism of the scene and can proceed to conjure up a demassified world that's behind-the-scene.

201展間／R201

單頻道錄像｜16 分鐘｜2022 年
Single-channel video｜16 min.｜2022

● 圖片提供：何采柔
● Photo credit: Joyce Ho

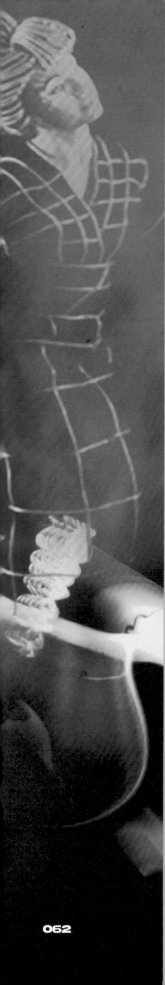

埃里卡・貝克曼
ERICKA BECKMAN

《中斷》
Hiatus

作品《中斷》描繪了一場發生於線上遊戲——「身分」中的冒險經歷。主角瑪迪於遊戲裡化身為牛仔，如同一個童話故事常有的情節一般，瑪迪的冒險旅程面臨困難、險阻、欺騙與迷惑，乃至力量遭受剝奪。藝術家在這個略帶復古氣質的數位遊戲裡將問題直面於觀眾：身處在這個被構建的系統中，我們所扮演的角色是什麼？而我們又該如何在此世界中保持我們的身分？在日常生活與遊戲介面愈難以分割，在生活與文化愈趨「遊戲化」、「娛樂化」抑或「樂園化」的世界中，她的作品藉由分析、展示這些系統及其策略，雖距離創作拍攝的時序已相隔 20 餘年，許多問題卻仍真實且值得玩味。

Hiatus presents an online "identity" adventure game. The main character, Wanda, is transformed into a go-go cowgirl in the game and makes her way through the game world. In typical fairy tale fashion, she encounters various troubles, obstacles, deceits, and confusion. Her power is even taken away from her. Through this rather retro-looking video game, the artist forces the audience to question the roles we play in constructed systems, and how we can maintain our identities in such worlds. As everyday life becomes increasingly more indistinguishable from the interface of a game and in a world where life and culture are becoming more gamified, entertainment-oriented, and amusement park-esque, the various issues raised in the analysis and display of such systems and strategies presented in this work created by Ericka Beckman over two decades ago remain valid and interesting today.

201 展間／R201
雙頻道錄像與燈光裝置、16 釐米膠卷轉 HD｜20 分 30 秒｜1999/2015 年
Dual screen installation with sequenced lighting, 16mm transferred to HD file｜20 min. 30 sec.｜1999/2015

● 圖片提供：埃里卡・貝克曼
● Photo credit: Ericka Beckman

導演、攝影、剪輯、製作：埃里卡・貝克曼
聲音設計：Bruce Darby
演員：Madi Distefano、Daniel Ruth
Produced, directed, shot, and edited by Ericka Beckman
Sound Design: Bruce Darby
Starring: Madi Distefano and Daniel Ruth

創作贊助：The National Endowment for the Arts, Massachusetts Council on the Arts, New York State Council on the Arts, and the Experimental Television Center.
Produced with funds from The National Endowment for the Arts, Massachusetts Council on the Arts, New York State Council on the Arts, and the Experimental Television Center.

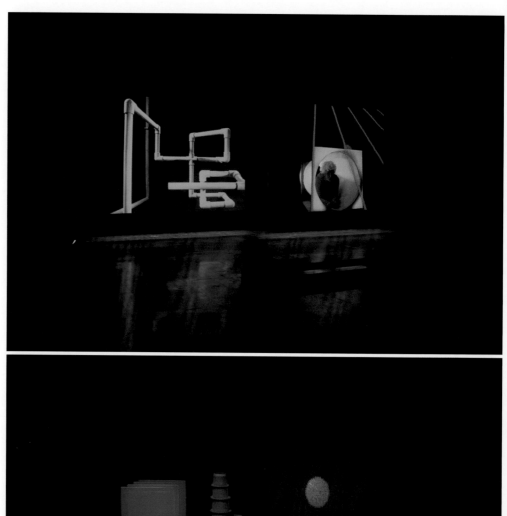

張允菡
CHANG YUN-HAN

《你是否曾夢見這樣的地方？》／《美國夢》
Have you ever dreamed of this place? / American Dream

此二件作品組合展出的是人類欲望於需求及滿足間的競合。作品《你是否曾夢見這樣的地方》以 1986 年的動畫《美國鼠譚》為基礎，在那傳說中沒有貓且遍地都是乳酪的他方幻象中，藝術家以每日紀實的報紙貼合《美國鼠譚》創造的生活幻象，問問什麼是對於美好未來的信仰？而作品《美國夢》則是藝術家通過對於紐約的觀察筆記，以魔術作為類比，描繪立基於自由與可能性的想望下，所創造出的大型都市幻術，讓幻術中生活的人們在快樂與愉悅的滿足情緒下，務實且積極地生存。此兩件作品利用一個類似「家」的積木造型結構，採取販賣生活出口與救贖的畸形秀設定，在幻象於屋外，幻術於屋內的展出中，暗示信仰與夢想在需求與滿足的內容設計下，也可被操作成可供調控的心靈工程。

The combination of the two works delineates the coopetition between the need and satisfaction of human desire. The work, *Have you ever dreamed of this place?*, builds upon the 1986 animation, *An American Tail*. This fantasy about an elsewhere place tells the legendary land where cats are non-existence, and cheese can be found everywhere. The artist incorporates real daily newspaper with the illusionary life From *An American Tail* to question the belief in a better future. In comparison, through the artist's observation notes on New York, *American Dream* uses magic as an analogy to describe the large-scale urban illusion that is built upon the desire for freedom and possibility, allowing people to live pragmatically and actively fight for survival under this joyous illusion. The works are brought together with a structure that looks like a "home" made out of building blocks. Packaged as a freak show peddling an outlet and salvation of life, illusions are displayed without the house, whereas illusory tricks are performed within, hinting that the need and satisfaction of beliefs and dreams can be a form of content design and manipulated into adjustable mind engineering.

201展間／R201
《你是否曾夢見這樣的地方？》 *Have you ever dreamed of this place?*
報紙、壓克力、水泥漆、水性麥克筆｜2022 年
Newspaper, acrylic, cement paint and water marker｜2022

《美國夢》 *American Dream*
雙頻道錄像｜7 分 49 秒｜2018 年
Dual screen｜7 min. 49 sec.｜2018

專輯執行

發行者｜財團法人台北市文化基金會
總編輯｜駱麗真
美術編輯｜陳彥如、魏妏如
展場攝影｜王世邦
翻譯｜廖蕙芬、游騰緯、黃亮融、謝雨珊

出版者｜財團法人台北市文化基金會台北當代藝術館
地址｜103 臺北市大同區長安西路 39 號
電話｜+886-2-2552-3721
傳真｜+886-2-2559-3874
網址｜www.mocataipei.org.tw
印刷｜奇異多媒體印藝有限公司
定價｜新臺幣 850 元
初版｜2023 年 12 月
ISBN｜978-626-96983-6-3

本專刊編輯著作權屬於臺北市政府文化局所有
翻印必究 ©

Editorial Team

Publisher: Taipei Culture Foundation
Chief Editor: Li-Chen Loh
Designers: Yanru Chen, Wenru Wei
Photographer: Anpis Wang
Translators: Hui-Fen Anna Liao, Tony Yu,
Liang-jung Huang, Catherine Y. Hsieh

Published by Taipei Culture Foundation / Museum of
Contemporary Art, Taipei
Address: No. 39, Chang-An West Road, Taipei, Taiwan
Telephone: +886-2-2552-3721
Fax: +886-2-2559-3874
Website: www.mocataipei.org.tw
Printed by CHIYI MEDIA PRINTING CO., LTD.
Price: TWD 850
First Published in December, 2023
ISBN: 978-626-96983-6-3

Copyright by the Department of Cultural Affairs, Taipei
City Government, all rights reserved.

指導單位
Supervisor

台北市文化局

主辦單位
Organizers

台北市文化基金會
Taipei Culture Foundation

台北當代藝術館
MoCA TAIPEI

贊助單位
Sponsors

THERMOS.

當代藝術基金會
Contemporary Art Foundation

財團法人
紀慧能藝術文化基金會

royal inn 老爺會館

年度指定投影機
Annual Sponsor for
Appointed Projector

EPSON
EXCEED YOUR VISION

年度指定電視／螢幕
Annual Sponsor for
Appointed TV / Screen

SONY

媒體協力
Media Cooperation

Rti 中央廣播電臺
Radio Taiwan International

特別感謝
Special Thanks

飛建中

國立臺北藝術大學
Taipei National University of the Arts

KdMoFA 關渡美術館
Kuandu Museum of Fine Arts

Federal Ministry
Republic of Austria
Arts, Culture,
Civil Service and Sport

共識覺：主題樂園幻想工程挑戰賽＝ The proto-ocean for co-
consciousness : making worlds an imagineering project ／駱
麗真總編輯・──初版・──臺北市：財團法人臺北市文化基金會
臺北當代藝術館出版：財團法人臺北市文化基金會發行，2023.12
　面；　公分
中英對照
ISBN 978-626-96983-6-3（平裝）

1.CST: 數位藝術 2.CST: 數位媒體 3.CST: 作品集

956.7   112021074